Library of Congress Cataloging-in-Publication Data available.

ISBN 978-1-4521-7031-2

Manufactured in China.

FSC
www.fsc.org
MIX
Paper from
responsible sources
FSC™ C008047

Design by Amelia Mack.
Typeset in Hightower.
The illustrations in this book were rendered in colored pencil.

10 9 8 7 6 5 4 3 2 1

Chronicle Books LLC
680 Second Street
San Francisco, California 94107

Chronicle Books—we see things differently. Become part of
our community at www.chroniclekids.com.

JE
RUE

RedLOCKS
and the Three Bears

Claudia Rueda

chronicle books · san francisco

12·27·2021

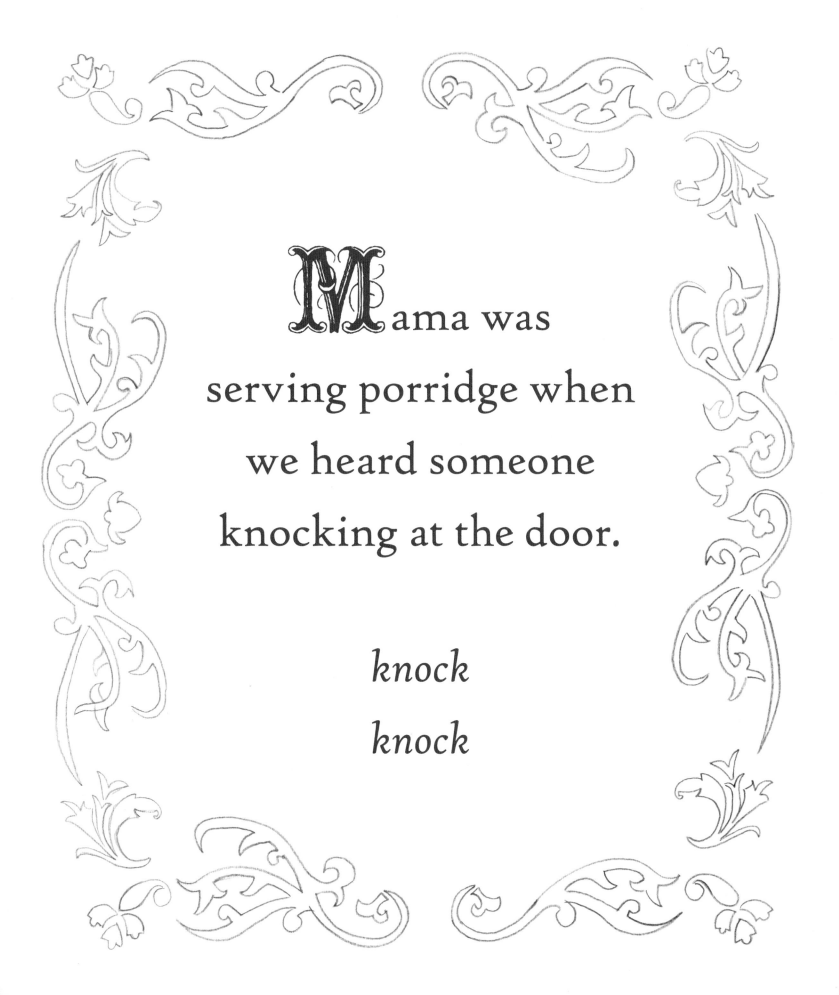

Mama was serving porridge when we heard someone knocking at the door.

knock

knock

Little Red from the book next door was asking for help.

There's a Big Bad Wolf in my book, and he wants to eat me. Please help!

Please . . .

I asked Papa and Mama

to let her stay.

Not sure if that's
how the story goes,
they said.

But . . .

OK.

Little Red was so
hungry she ate all
my porridge!

mmmmmm

Then she broke my favorite chair while telling us about the Big Bad Wolf.

It was getting late,
so I told her she
could use my bed.

ZZZZZZ

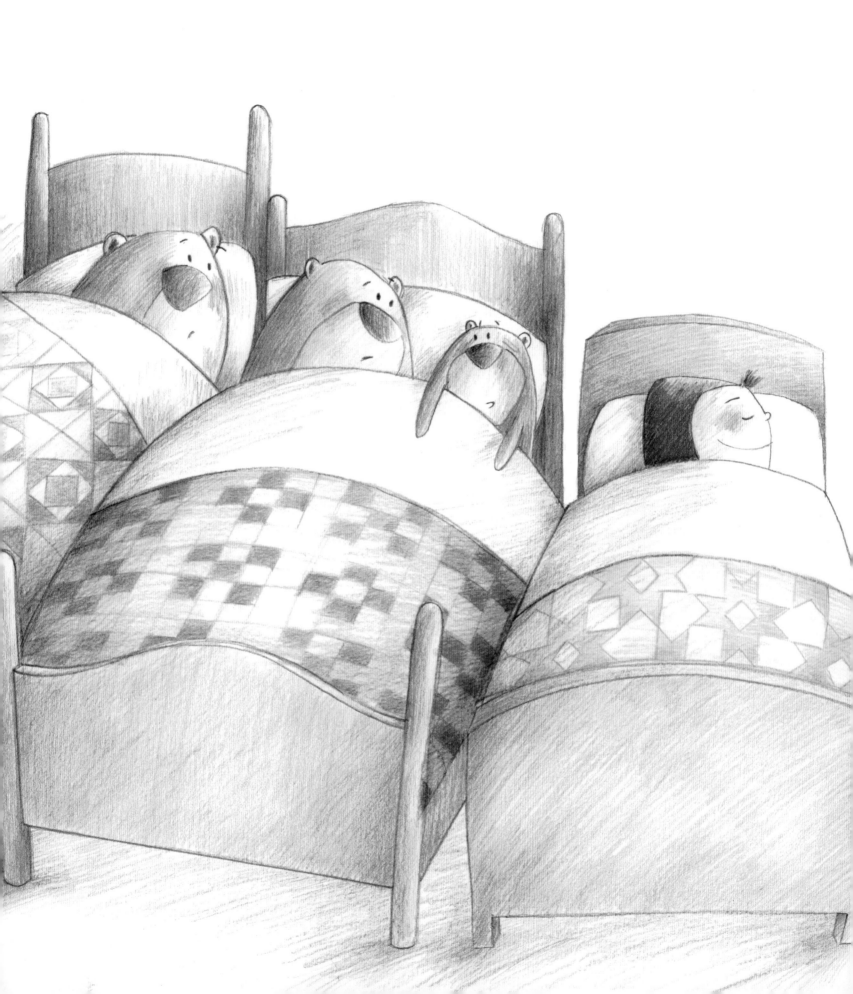

I couldn't sleep
because Mama's bed
was too soft. That's
when I saw . . .

Uh-oh!

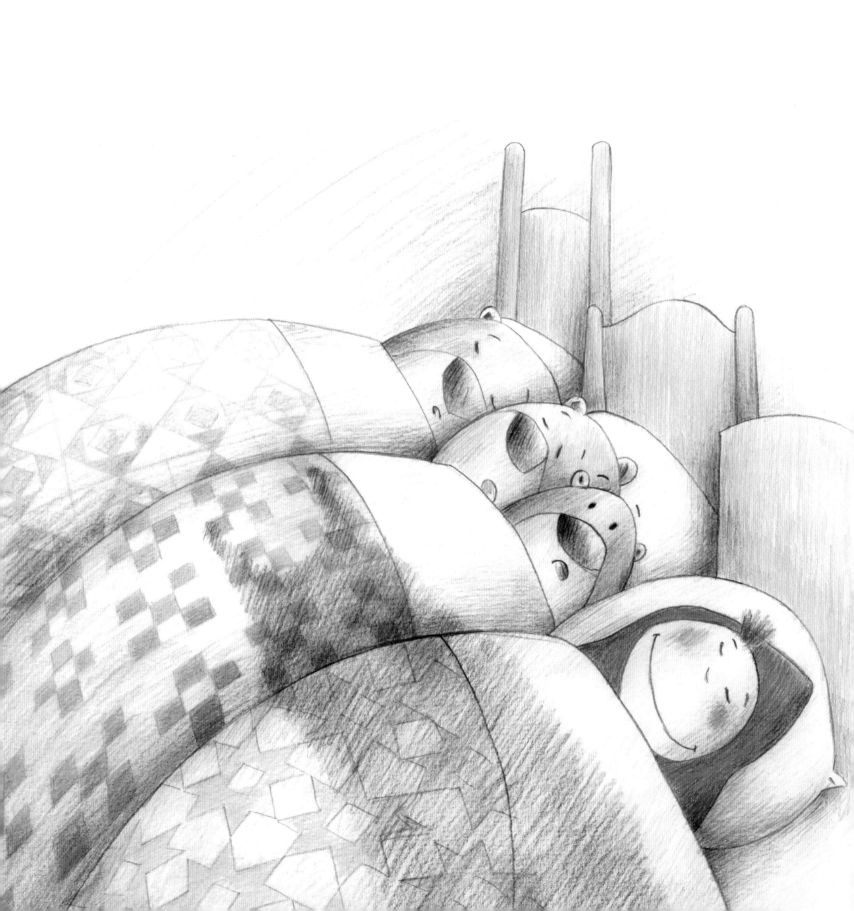

The wolf!

We ran to another book to stay
away from the wolf.

!!!

It's him, the wolf from my book!
Little Red said.

Then we heard someone
whining, so I decided
to take a look.

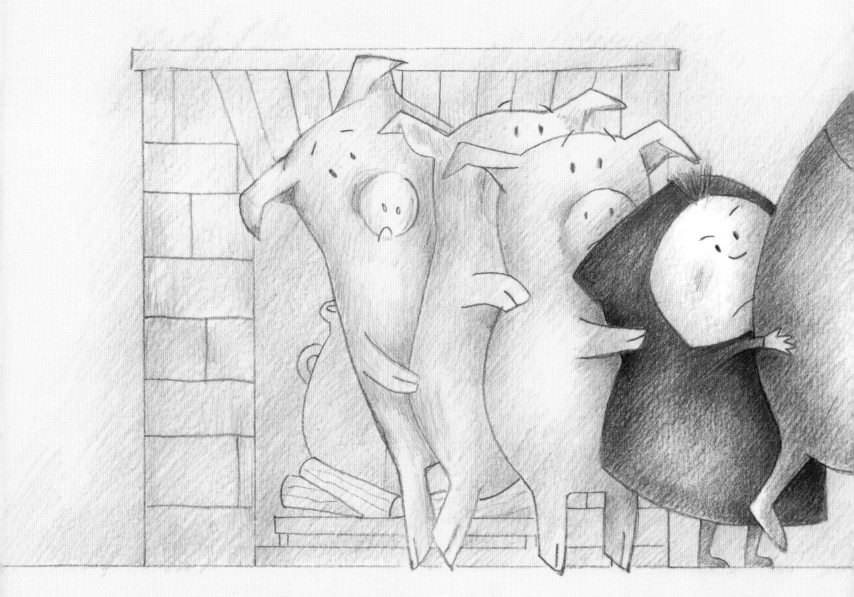

Buahhh!

It was the wolf who was crying!

Nobody likes to have wolves in their books. I don't want to be the Big Bad Wolf anymore.

So I had an idea! I asked Wolf
to come downstairs and offered
him a bowl of hot porridge.

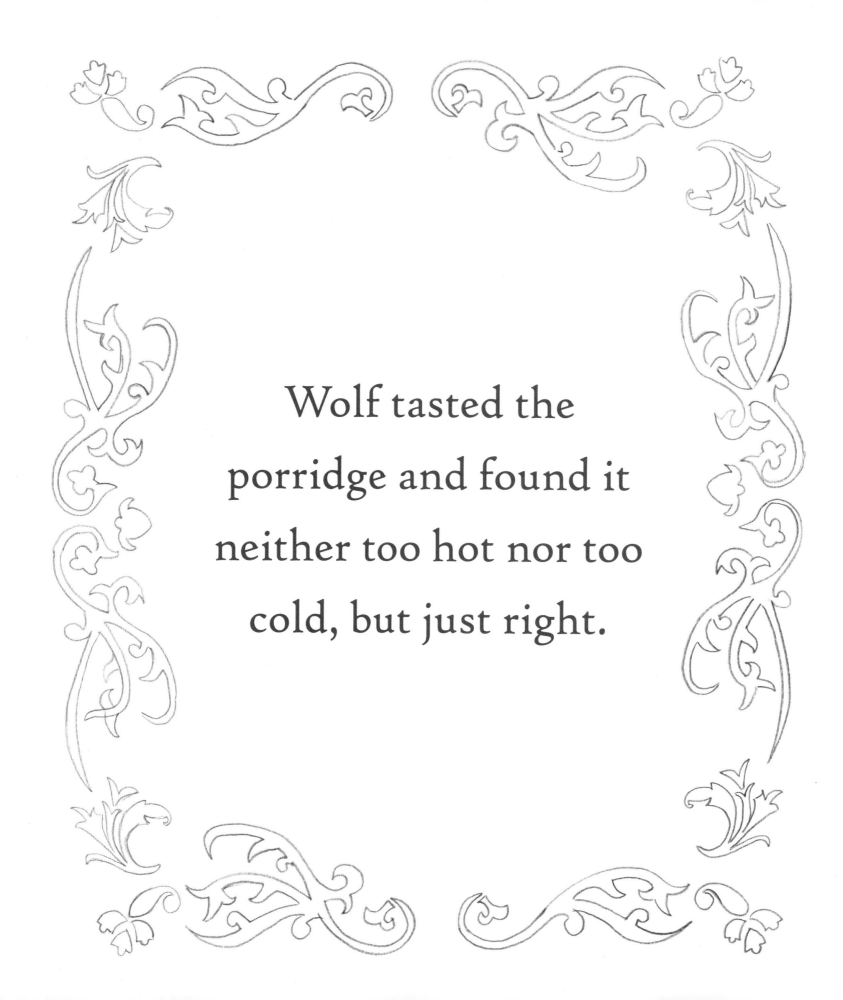

Wolf tasted the porridge and found it neither too hot nor too cold, but just right.

He liked it so well

that he ate it all up,

every bit!

And then asked

for more.

After Wolf had three bowls,
I measured his mouth

to show Little Red it was not big
and terrible, but just right.

They both returned
to their book.

Little Red took some
porridge for Grandma,
and Wolf wrote down
Mama's secret recipe.

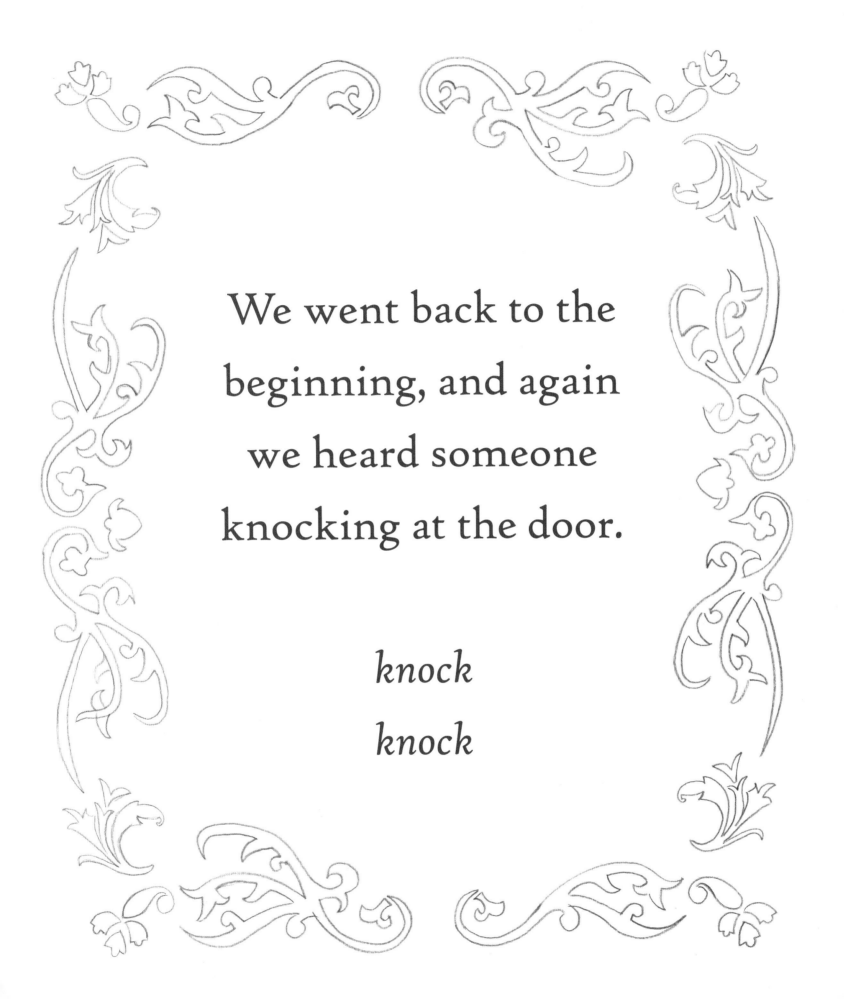

We went back to the beginning, and again we heard someone knocking at the door.

knock

knock

I think we've had
enough visitors
for now,
said Mama.

Let's lock
the door and eat our
porridge.

Who's Goldilocks?
We've never heard
of her.

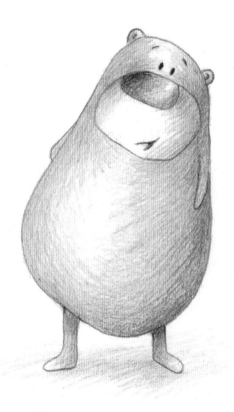

Mama's Porridge
secret recipe

- 1 cup of oats
- 1 cup of milk
- 1 cup of water
- A pinch of salt
- 1 teaspoon of cinnamon ← secret ingredient
- 1 tablespoon of honey

Mix all in a saucepan and simmer for 4 minutes.